Missing
My Best Friend

Written By Norma Thorstad Knapp

Illustrated By Faythe Mills

For my grandson Brandon and in memory of my sister, Evie.
And also for my other grandchildren, Julia, Kryst, and Madeline. - NTK

For my best friends, Egan, Demi, Alayna, Grayson, and Canon.
And in memory of my mother and father, Audrey and Donald Thomas. - FM

Acknowledgements:
The author wishes to thank Barb Johnson, Caroline Kowis, Connie Schmidt,
Deb Mercier, Gretchen Nelson, Jack Rustan, Julie Paulson, Karen Arm,
Kathy Munsch, Mary Hammargren, and Patricia Conner.

Both the author and the artist extend heartfelt appreciation to models
Julie and Jamie Loken and their children Michael, Christopher, and Grace,
and Grandparents Michael and Ginny Loken.

Second Printing 2012
ISBN 978-0-9846314-0-7
Printed and bound by Sentinel Printing, St. Cloud, MN, USA
The pictures in this book were done in soft pastels.
"Where the Wild Things Are" mentioned on page 18 was written and illustrated by Maurice Sendak.

Summary: A story about the power of friendship between two young boys, the subsequent grief
when one boy dies, and the importance of a family's love.

SpringJoy Press
Alexandria, MN

A NOTE FOR PARENTS AND TEACHERS

When children die, we adults are faced with challenging dilemmas. We may ask ourselves: Should other children be told what happened? Will hiding or altering the truth protect or possibly harm? We can get so caught up in our own grief we forget that the children's friends may be grieving too.

There is no one right way to help children who experience the death of someone close. One vehicle may be the reading of a book, such as this one, with them. Young children often cannot fully grasp the concept of death; thus, we adults need to lay the foundation for more understanding.

There is no need to go into more detail than is necessary or can be understood. Assure them that nothing they've said or wished or done has contributed to the person's death in any way. Also, provide escape time to give them opportunities to interact with other children and times to leave the sadness that can surround a death.

Take your cues from the children regarding how much information to give. They may ask the same questions over and over. This is part of the process that helps them cope with something that is confusing and/or frightening. Honesty, simplicity, and receptivity are key components. Let them cry, and let them simply feel how they feel.

It's difficult for most children to express their emotions in words. When they do, acknowledge, validate, and support them. Giving children opportunities to express and share their feelings with the adults they love and depend on helps them work through their fears and confusion. Let them know that nothing is too sad or too terrible to talk about. A warm tone of voice will do much to reassure children who are trying to assimilate painful ideas. Using this book can also help explain how you, the adult, feel and can begin the process of healing and commemorating the one who has died.

Jack and I were best friends.

We met in the spring
when my family moved to a small town.

We used to live in an apartment.
It was far away in the big city.

Our new house
was two stories high.
I was happy
when I saw the tire swing
in the back yard.

The family next door had two kids:
a boy named Jack and his little sister Lacey.
Jack was eight years old, and I was seven.
From their porch, they watched us carry boxes.
Some were very heavy!

Jack and I liked that we looked almost the same.
We were almost the same size.
When we stood back to back and measured,
Jack was just a little bit taller.

Jack and I both had blue eyes.
We both had light brown hair.
Jack had some tiny freckles across his nose.
His mom called them angel kisses.
We liked to wear T-shirts and blue jeans.
And Jack always wore black tennis shoes.

Our houses even looked the same.
Both of them had wide front porches.
They were both painted light colors.
Mine was blue; Jack's was green.
Our back yards were filled with
lots of big oak and maple trees.

When school started, we liked
to sit together in the front seat on the school bus.
We were in the same room at school.

In the wintertime
we rode on our dads' snowmobiles.
We sat on the seats behind them.
We liked to go fast. On every ride,
they would remind us, "Hang on real tight!"

Jack's mouth was behind his face mask,
but I could tell by his eyes
that he was smiling--just like me.

Spring was our favorite season.
We planted flower seeds
in pots for our front porches.
We worked while the birds sang.
Our noses itched from the smell of oil
when we helped my dad fix his old yellow car.

We learned how to swim that summer.
Jack liked to go swimming in pools;
I liked to swim in lakes.

We liked lots of the same things.
We liked the gooey taste
of extra cheese pizza and its yummy smells.

My mom and dad bought me
a brand new red bike for my birthday.
I couldn't have one in the big city.
Dad taught me how to ride it.
Jack helped me when I tipped over and fell down.
He was a good friend.

In the fall we helped our dads
rake leaves into huge piles.
Some leaves were red. Some were yellow.
Some were orange.
They were different sizes, shapes, and colors
and made lots of noise when we played in them.

One fall day a large leaf pile we'd made wiggled.
Dad said, "What do you think is in that pile
of leaves?!" It was Jack's sister, Lacey!
We laughed so hard we
fell into the leaf pile.
It felt crunchy like
playing in an enormous
bowl of cereal!

Jack and I liked silly riddles.
We liked knock-knock jokes.
We liked to read books.
Our favorite book was "Where the Wild Things Are."
Best of all, we liked each other.

The last time I saw my best friend
we were upstairs in my bedroom.
We had been playing.
Everything outside was cold and white with snow.
My windows were full of snowflake patterns.

There was an accident,
and my *best* friend died that winter.

"Accidents sometimes happen," Dad told me.
"And sometimes people die in an accident.
When *somebody* dies,
their body just stops working."

I felt very, very sad when my best friend died.

Pizza didn't taste good anymore.
And I wanted my mom to drive me to school.

I didn't like Legos or my bike, either.
And my stomach hurt
whenever I thought of my best friend.

Sometimes I had bad dreams.
Sometimes I cried.
Mom would rub my back
and tell me, "When you feel sad,
it's okay to cry.
Tears help wash away
the hurt and the sadness."

Dad told me that it's a sad
and scary time for all of us.
He said, "I feel scared, mad, and sad too.
And sometimes I feel confused."
Then he said, "We will help each other
get through this."

Grandma said,
"We shouldn't be alone at this time.
We need to be with family and friends.
We need their smiles, their laps,
and their hugs."

Grandpa helped me make a
"Memory Book."
It's all about Jack.

When I feel sad and miss my best friend,
I look at it. It's filled with pictures
of Jack and things he liked:
Legos, sunflowers, lambs, and lizards.

Grandma helped me make a quilt about Jack.
First, we drew pictures of things he liked.
Next, we painted the pictures with fabric paints.

Then Grandma sewed the pieces together.
While we were working, she said,
"When we hurt, God hurts too."

Mom reminds me that
Jack will always be with me.
She says the memory of him will
always be right here in my heart.
She says that life ends,
but love does not.

Norma Thorstad Knapp grew up in western North Dakota, Idaho, and Oregon. Her family moved often, giving her a rich foundation for writing. After college, she worked as a registered nurse, educator, crisis counselor, youth specialist, and bereavement facilitator in cities in North Dakota, Texas, and Minnesota. She has published numerous stories, essays and poems; several short stories and a sermon have won awards. Her days are full with reading, writing, traveling, time with grandchildren, creating note cards, and hospice volunteer bereavement work. She has a grown daughter and son and four grandchildren.
www.normaKnapp.com

Faythe Mills is a graphic artist living in Glenwood, Minnesota, on beautiful Lake Minnewaska. Although she works with a variety of mediums, pastels are her favorite when illustrating. She has also illustrated 'The Captain's Hat' and 'The Adventures of Molly & Skunky' for Deb Mercier. She has been blessed with two sons and five grandchildren. Her artwork and books can be found at:
www.mnartists.org/faythe__mills
www.faythemills.com
www.minnewaskapress.com